Priscilla and Rosy

For Allison Blum
S J

FOR THE GROUP OF EIGHT, PLUS ONE
L H

Text copyright © 2001 by Sharon Jennings
Illustrations copyright © 2001 by Linda Hendry

Published in Canada by Fitzhenry & Whiteside,
195 Allstate Parkway, Markham, Ontario L3R 4T8

Published in the United States by Fitzhenry & Whiteside,
121 Harvard Avenue, Suite 2, Allston, Massachusetts 02134

Printed in Hong Kong

10 9 8 7 6 5 4 3 2 1

National Library of Canada Cataloguing in Publication Data

Jennings, Sharon
Priscilla and Rosy

ISBN 1-55041-676-6

I. Hendry, Linda   II. Title.

PS8569.E563P75 2001   jC813'.54   C2001-901082-6
PZ7.J429877Pr 2001

U.S. Cataloging-in-Publication Data
(Library of Congress Standards)

Jennings, Sharon.
Priscilla and Rosy / by Sharon Jennings ; illustrated by Linda Hendry. –1st ed.
[32] p. : col. ill. ; cm.
Summary: A tempting boat trip tests an alley-rat's loyalty to her best friend.
IBSN 1-55041-6766
1. Best friends -- Fiction. I. Hendry, Linda, ill. II. Title.
[E] 21 2001 AC   CIP

Fitzhenry & Whiteside acknowledges with thanks the Canada Council for the Arts,
the Government of Canada through the Book Publishing Industry Development Program (BPIDP),
and the Ontario Arts Council for their support of our publishing program.

Design by Wycliffe Smith

Priscilla and Rosy

By Sharon Jennings

Illustrated by Linda Hendry

Fitzhenry & Whiteside

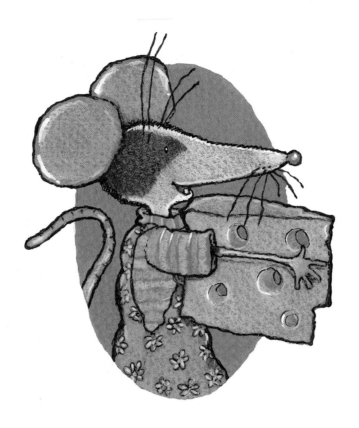

Priscilla lived in an alley behind a restaurant.
Her home was a hole in the loose bricks hidden by the
garbage cans. Priscilla's best friend, Rosy, lived across the
gutter, near the ice cream store.

On Sunday night, Priscilla met Rosy at their usual spot.
They had worked hard all week, running back and forth
from the restaurants to their homes, carrying scraps of
food and scaring lots of people. Tomorrow was Monday,
and Priscilla and Rosy always took Monday off.

"Will you come to my place tomorrow?" asked Rosy.
"I've got a new puzzle."

"I'll be there first thing," promised Priscilla.

Her phone was ringing as Priscilla reached home.
It was Rudolph.

"My uncle's taking me on his boat tomorrow,"
he said. "And I can bring a friend. Will you come?"

"Oh yes!" exclaimed Priscilla. "I've never been
on a boat."

"Come early," said Rudoph.

"I'll be there first thing," promised Priscilla.

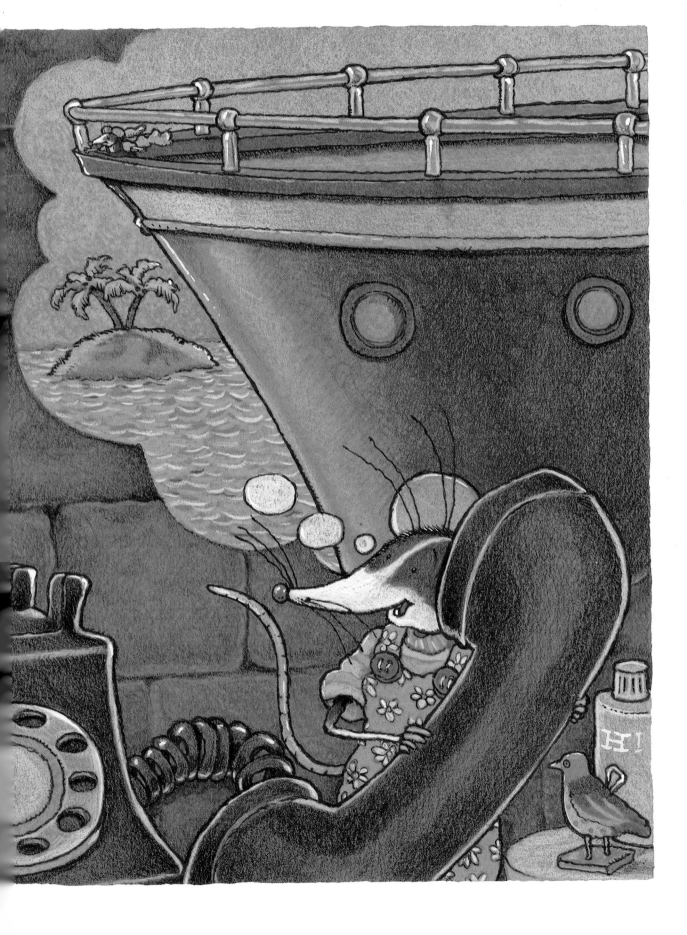

Priscilla was too excited to sit still. She pushed aside a brick and ran outside.

"What is it, Priscilla?" asked Cuthbert. "Why are you so happy?"

"I'm going on a boat with Rudolph," Priscilla answered. "First thing tomorrow morning."

"But I heard you make plans with Rosy," replied Cuthbert.

"Oh, pooh," said Priscilla. "I can do Rosy's puzzle any old time."

"Some friend you are," snorted Cuthbert.

Priscilla frowned.

"I'll phone Rosy tomorrow and tell her I'm sick,"
said Priscilla.

"That's a fib," replied Cuthbert.

"Then I'll tell her I forgot I was already busy."

"Priscilla Rat, you are not nice!" declared Cuthbert.

Priscilla stuck out her tongue.

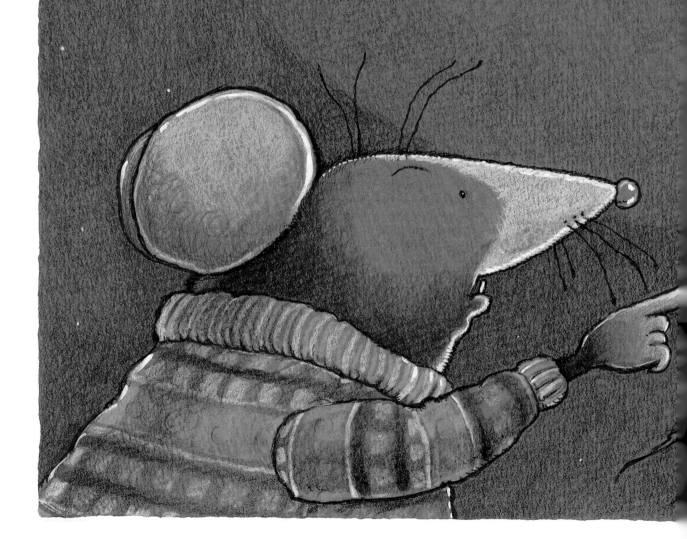

Priscilla ran back home. She pushed and shoved her bricks until she was all closed in.

"Not fair!" she yelled, kicking her chair.

"I want to go on a boat!" she yelled even louder, and kicked her bed.

"I hate puzzles!" she yelled at the top of her lungs.

Priscilla looked around for something else to kick.

Instead, Priscilla saw the photograph of Rosy and her holding hands and smiling. That was the day of the horrible storm. Rosy had pulled her out of the sewer and saved her life.

Priscilla sighed and sat down. She knew she could never be mean to Rosy. She phoned Rudolph and told him the truth.

The next morning, Priscilla awoke bright and early. Right after breakfast, she hurried along the gutter to Rosy's. She gave the secret knock and heard Rosy call from inside.

"I phoned and just missed you, Priscilla," Rosy moaned.
"I feel sick and can't play."

Priscilla shrieked, "You can't be sick! What about
the puzzle?"

But Rosy just moaned again.

Priscilla moaned too.

Priscilla trudged back through the gutter. But halfway
home, she had an idea. Maybe it wasn't too late to call
Rudolph. Maybe she could still go on the boat. Priscilla
began to skip. She felt so happy, she even managed to
smile at Winston's noisy new babies.

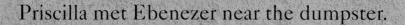

Priscilla met Ebenezer near the dumpster.

"Guess what?" said Ebenezer. "I'm going on a boat
with Rudolph!"

"Oh, rats," grumbled Priscilla.

"I've been on lots of boats," added Ebenezer.
"It's fun."

Priscilla scowled and stomped off.

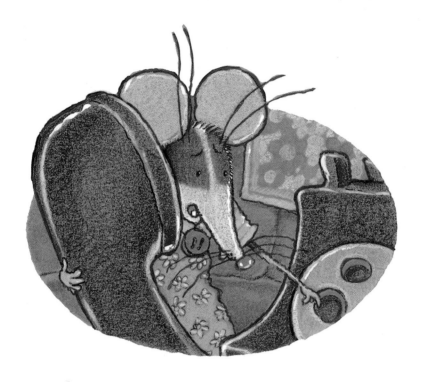

Priscilla reached home, grumpy and tired. She phoned her other friends, but everyone was busy. She went all alone to the movie theatre, but it was a show she'd already seen.

At last it was suppertime, and Priscilla got out pots and pans.

"This has been the worst Monday ever," she declared. "It couldn't have been worse, unless...unless...." Priscilla stopped to think.

"Unless I was sick in bed and all alone," she finished.

Priscilla got out her knapsack and filled it with her tastiest scraps. She lugged it along the gutter down the alley to Rosy's.

She went straight in and sat down by Rosy's bed.

And when Rosy woke up, Priscilla spoon-fed her a nourishing supper and read her their favorite book.

"Thank you for coming," said Rosy. "You are a very good friend."

Priscilla smiled. "Yes, I am," she agreed.